JAKE,

Happy Reading!

We love you –

XO

GRANDMA

+

Grandpa

To my husband, Norman, and daughters, Jennifer and Emily - thanks for encouraging me to publish this book and for being so patient during the process. I love our life in Naples.

To the Hunt family, thank you for starting me on my Naples journey, and to my sister, Karen, thank you for all your guidance. To the rest of my family and friends - thanks for all your support, kind words and genuine excitement about my book. You helped me make my dream a reality.

To those who live in Naples, we are so lucky to call this beautiful place home. To those who visit, we are thrilled to share with you a little piece of paradise.

-L.T.

N is for Naples

Requests for permission to make copies of any part of the work should be submitted online at info@mascotbooks.com or mailed to Mascot Books, 560 Herndon Parkway, Suite #120, Herndon, VA 20170

PRT0614C

Printed in the United States.

ISBN-13: 978-1-937406-19-6
ISBN-10: 1-937406-19-9

www.mascotbooks.com

N is for NAPLES

Lisa Trebilcock

illustrated by
Cheri Nowak

is for alligator
In the back lake
Sunning on the bank
My sister named him Jake.

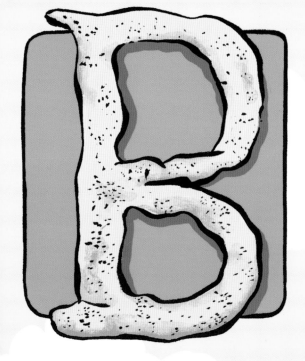

is for beach
Stretching for miles
Castles look best
Built from sand piles.

C is for coconuts
Hanging so high
Snap off and plop
Smack into the tide.

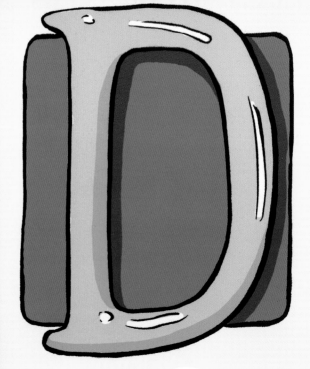

is for dolphins
Oh how they play
Jumping and diving
Watch them all day.

is for egret
Tall at the shore
He loves to eat fish
I think he's had four!

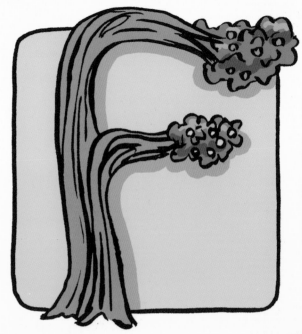

is for fruit trees
Lemon and lime
Grapefruit and oranges
Pick one at a time.

is for the Gulf
Of Mexico, so blue
Boat, fish and swim
All fun things to do.

is for hammock
Rocks me to sleep
Can't move too quickly
I'll land in a heap!

is for island
We anchor off shore
Become treasure hunters
It's so fun to explore.

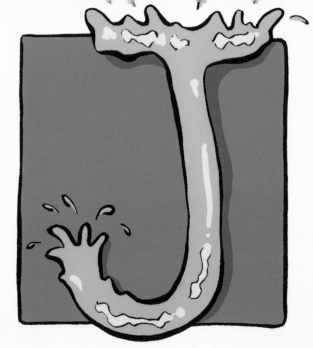

is for jumping
Safely off my dock
Aim for the deep spot
And don't hit a rock!

is for kayak
Gliding along
Clear waters so still
Arms so strong.

is for lions
We see at Naples Zoo
My mom likes the giraffes
I like them, too.

We went!
😊

M

is for manatee
Gentle sea cow of the south
Big tail like a paddle
Small whiskers on its snout.

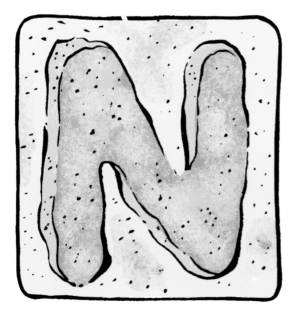

is for Naples
The best place to be
Easy tropical living
Nestled nicely by the sea.

is for oysters
Tucked in their beds
Growing on mangrove roots
Crabs stepping on their heads!

is for pelican
Perched on the pier
Catching fish in his pouch
He stands so near.

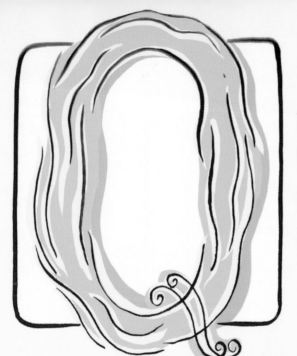

is for quiet
Palm trees as they sway
Light breeze over the water
Gentle waves on Naples Bay.

is for ramps
At the skateboard park
Skate all year long
Even after dark.

is for sunset
Orange ball aglow
Melting into the horizon
Moving so slow.

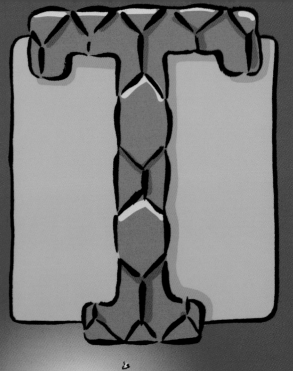

is for turtle
Crawls ashore by moonlight
Makes tracks up the beach
Builds her nest in the night.

is for under
The sea, so dark
Diving down deep
Look - it's a shark!

is for vacation
Climb the banyan tree
At the Golisano Children's Museum
So much in Naples to see.

is for winter
Visitors love to play
Golf, tennis, surfing
Try a new sport each day.

is for extra
Letters I will need
So much fun in Naples
So much fun, indeed.

is for you
Reading this book
All about Naples
Come have a look!

Z is for zzzzz
It's bedtime for me
Another day in Naples
Awesome as can be.

The End

What have you seen in Naples?

- ☐ Alligator
- ☐ Coconut
- ☐ Dolphin
- ☐ Giraffe
- ☐ Manatee

When you see it, check it off.

☐ Pelican

☐ Crab

☐ Sunset

☐ Sand Castle

☐ 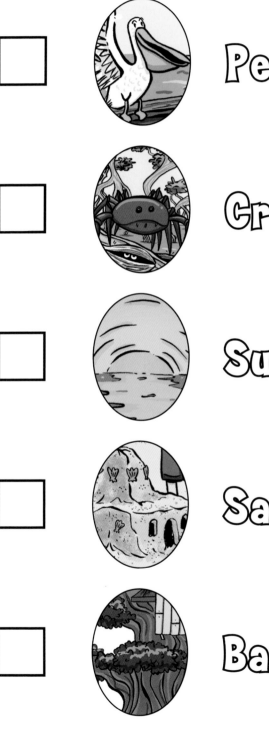 Banyan Tree

Lisa Trebilcock:

Lisa graduated with a Bachelor's Degree in Journalism from Northeastern University in Boston. Tired of New England winters, she relocated to Naples over 20 years ago. Lisa has volunteered over 3,000 hours at Sea Gate Elementary School, and has been honored by the school district in its "Galaxy of Stars."

Cheri Nowak:

Cheri studied cartooning and illustration at the School of Visual Arts in New York City, and is currently studying Communication Design at the Fashion Institute of Technology. She's lived on Long Island her entire life and loves being close to both the beach and the city. Besides drawing, she enjoys sci-fi, reading, cake decorating, movies and spending time with her friends and family.